Y0-BQH-487

Doggerel

An attempt by the author to revive a type of literature prevalent in England three or four centuries ago. The few people who could read, would have read it in early "newspapers" such as The Spectator. The illiterates would have heard it *sung* by the traveling troubadours.

Doggerel often contained a hidden message that, if written undisguised, would have caused heads to roll. Its use subjected those in power to ridicule, and eventually helped to expose the abuse of the illiterates by those in power.

Read on and decide whether these conditions may be happening again.

DISCARD

WEST GEORGIA REGIONAL LIBRARY SYSTEM

Doggerel

A personal publication by author, George M. Henzel and Cartoonist, Carol Moretti.

Printing history

Published by: 'by george' Publications

All rights reserved.
Copyright © 1987 by George M. Henzel and Carol Moretti. This book may not be reproduced in whole or in part by mimeograph or any other means, without permission. For information address: 'by george' Publications, P.O. Box 172, Mt. Horeb, WI 53572.

ISBN 0-942611-00-4

Printed in the United States of America.

DISCLAIMER

All names, faces, people, characters, institutions, concerns, occupations, organizations and situations herein are fictional in nature and are not to be associated with any real or imagined names, faces, people, characters, institutions, concerns, occupations, organizations or situations. Any similarity to actual conditions is coincidental and was not implied or inferred.

ACKNOWLEDGMENTS

First. I want to express my gratitude to Carol Moretti, the Cartoonist, for her tremendous task of visualizing the meanings in the doggerel.

Second, the efforts of two persons, one successful—John Jones, and one unsuccessful, although doggedly determined, Steve Cummings, to search out and bring together the compilers of this volume.

And third, the host of friends, relatives, acquaintances, and just plain strangers who insisted that this material should be assembled into a book.

So, here it is!

DEDICATION

To dedicate this book to one person would be to slight a hundred. I therefore dedicate it to all and sundry who expressed a desire to see it in print. Enjoy!

᧒23691   WEST GEORGIA REGIONAL LIBRARY SYSTEM

Doggerel

INTRODUCTION

In the Standard Collegiate Dictionary, Doggerel is listed as "Trivial", awkwardly written verse, usually comic or burlesque". Good examples of *doggerel* known to every school child are, *Mary had a Little Lamb, Little Miss Muffet* and *Humpty Dumpty.*

You may, or may not, know that these and other Nursery Rhymes were written as satirical wit, to point out the often high-handed actions of the, then ruling, Aristocracy. Troubadours sang and the early newspapers, such as The Spectator, printed these pieces of doggerel. Although the wording of these verses appeared to be innocent indeed, everyone knew the message they carried.

Little, or none, of this type of doggerel appears in print today, and this volume is an attempt to bring back to life a type of literature so memorialized in those nursery rhymes.

Doggerel, like some food or drink, should not be taken in large doses. It is therefor recommended that it be read in small amounts at any one time, not gupled down in one reading.

What is the appeal of doggerel? First, the rhyming pleases the reader's ear. Second, the economy of words enables the reader to quickly absorb its meaning. Third, the *twisting* of phrases to achieve the rhyming lends enchantment. In this volume, a fourth appeal is attempted. That is, to bring another sense into play, in the form of a humorous cartoon to visually enforce the message carried in the rhyming doggerel.

The rhymes are by George M. Henzel, using the by-line, 'by george'. The difficult and excellent job of matching cartoons to the rhymes by Cartoonist, Carol Moretti. We hope that our efforts herein tickle your funny bone.

Inasmuch as there is no word for a single piece of doggerel except the awkward phrase, *a bit of doggerel,* each individual piece in this volume is dubbed a **PUPPEREL.**

INDEX

INDEX (Cont.)

SECTIONS

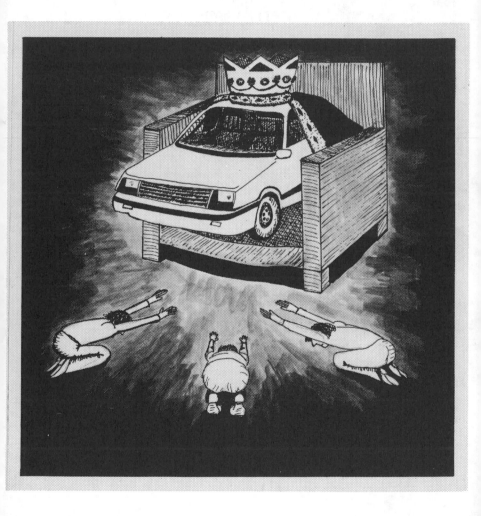

CARS

Belt — Schmelt

Buckle up? Buckle up?? Where have they been?
You're already buckled, in plastic and tin.
Used to be room, to swing a cat,
Now there's no space, for even a hat.

Cars'll soon be made, sized like a suit,
A forty-four long, or a twenty-two cute.
The car's exterior, it looks so stately,
Two people inside, and you breathe alterNATELY.

Reach for the buckle, you elbow your date.
Fasten that buckle, her eyes will dilate.
Eating in your car, is tempting fate.
Takes *Jaws-of-life,* your bod' to extricate.

Just squeezing in, is quite a hurdle,
Like a forty-four stout, in a thirty-two girdle.
There's so little room, you get claustro-phobia.
Belt in your belly, and you've got paranoia.

Oh seat belts are fine, and lives they save.
Wear them we should, from cradle to grave.
If someone could just, do some designing.
So belts wouldn't be, so d---- confining!

Don't limit me

Why in the world, did old Mother Nature,
People the world with, so stubborn a cray-ture?
Set him a limit, he'll fret and he'll stew,
And then exceed it, to *Hell* with you!

Now fifty-five miles, is enough per hour,
That anyone needs, to drive a car.
But this is a limit, that he can't abide!
To show his contempt, at sixty he'll ride.

No matter the figure, the Law had set,
He'd do five better, on that we'll bet.
Had we been wise, and fifty miles said,
He'd *DO* fifty-five, the old Bullhead.

A slow reflex, or brake out of adjust,
At only fifty-five, a gut you can bust.
Go sixty or more, you've brains of an *APE,*
It's off the highway, your body they'll scrape.

So if it's you, we're talking about here,
And your own safety, you don't hold dear.
Think of the others, whose roads you share,
Drive but fifty-five, and drive with care.

6

Hyperdention

The worst fears, that are devil sent,
Is the trepidation, before the first dent.
The dent, that is, in that bit'o perfection,
You just drove out, of the new car section.

There's dents and dents, all done accidentally,
But none to sear, your soul so intently,
As that very first mar, in your brand new car.
You'd gladly suffer it, in yourself, by far.

Your driving skill, is put to the test.
You're extra careful, on your behavior, best.
With every close call, you hold your breath.
If someone is close, you're scared to death.

Such apprehension, blood-pressure will hike,
Best get it over, and save your psyche.
For no extra charge, in the Dealer's shop,
A decorative dent, they'll gladly chop.

And with this demon, now off your back,
You can really enjoy, your brand new hack.
But should your actions, some questions bring,
Just claim innovation, the latest *in thing*.

Tell 'em you attended, a *dent and scratch* sale,
But your efforts to buy, were of no avail.
Till a salesman insisted, your wishes be sated,
And dented one up, while you sat and waited.

Plasticitis

Olds, Ford, Chrysler, Dodge, Studebaker.
All proudly bore, the name of their maker.
Built of steel and wood, as motor cars should.
Not ersatz and cardboard, or plastics no good.

But times did change, and in the rat-race hot,
Only car names with action, moved off the lot.
Now Charger, Now Jaguar, Now Pinto, Now Rover,
The name sold the car, while plastics took over.

With *ACTION* all spent, and *POWER* now king,
Mixed letters and numbers are really the thing.
It's 325e or 300TD, or Mark V11 or LSC
Or 5-Speed, 35 MPG, 2.8 liter or 500 SE

Onboard computers, headlights that wink,
Everything aboard, but a kitchen sink.
With weight to hold down, and milages to meet,
A throw-away plastic, will next hit the street.

Can you fix the toilet ? ?

The Wrench-Wrasslers

Wonder of wonders, of a miracle we speak.
And this one occurred, only last week.
In a suburban home, on the city's border,
Every last appliance, was in working order.

Both *fridge* and *freezer,* yea disposer and dryer.
And believe it or not, even de-humidifier.
The T.V. was TV*ing* the micro-wave *waving.*
But the biggest surprise, the plumbing *behaving.*

Outside the house, the drive seemed bare.
No wrench-wrassler's truck, was anchored there.
The garage door-opener, the door did 'ope.
Lawn mower started, first pull of the rope.

No note on the door, some repairman to direct,
To the neighbor's house, a key to collect.
EVERYTHING working, from A to Z!
Sure, we're pulling your leg, it's pure fantasy!

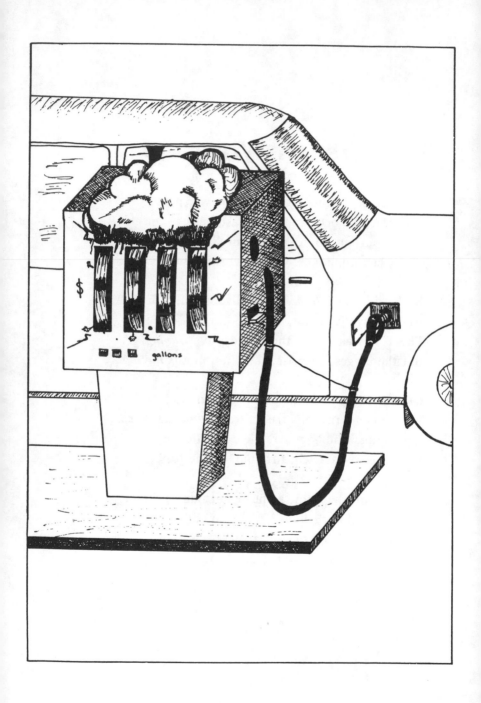

That Gas Pump

Oh, Time in its flight, is frightfully fast,
And a Rocket's speed, is likewise vast.
But they're slow as snails, or a jogger plump,
Compared to the wheels, on a gas station pump!

One set of wheels, calculating in tenths,
The other real busy, with dollars and cents.
Both, racing like mad, thier numbers clicking,
While OPEC over yonder, their chops are licking.

My eyes won't focus, my head it reels,
Got'a stop watchin', those spinning wheels.
My stomach's upset, *queezy,* I call it.
But what hurts most, is my shrinking wallet.

I stare and I stare, in utter fascination,
At those speeding wheels, and their wild gyration.
And just can't wait, for the nozzle to *WUMP,*
And *STOP* those wheels, on the Gas Station *PUMP.*

Time Bomb

Only thing worse, on a road than skunk,
Is an ignorant moron, driving while drunk.
Skunk on the road? It can but smell.
Drunk on the road, is unmitigated **HELL**.

Nigh unto a century, and the problem grows,
The millions we've spent? Lord only knows.
Educating this maniac, 'tis the wrong goal,
Like tossing money, down a rat hole.

Trying to pound sense, in to a closed mind,
Or push it beyond, its thirteen-year bind.
Is a sinful waste, of time and cash.
Like using your head, a stone wall to bash.

Much better by far, those millions we use,
And teach the others, who do not abuse,
To spot this menace, his path to avoid.
To treat him as though, he had Typhoid.

To know his traits, spot him from afar.
Stay out'a the way, of his wavering car.
Treat him the same, as a Tornado wild.
He's equally dangerous, and easily riled.

YOUR rights forfeit, small price to pay,
For the priviledge of living, yet another day.
Better to humor, this idiot sadistic,
Than stand your ground, and become a statistic.

Oh, give him wide berth, a lot'a room,
Let him rush on, to his inevitable doom.
Follow the course, we herein instruct,
Stay out'a his way, and he'll self-destruct!

Wheels

Of all the fears, that tear man's soul,
That chill one's blood, and take their toll.
There's none your body, with sweat will soak,
Like awaiting the verdict, from a garage's good-folk.

That noisy thump, that one only hears,
When rounding curves, or changing gears.
The stalling at lights, and — Oh, my Lord!
There's no more room, on Goody's clip board!

There's still the brakes, and the manifold too.
What in the world, am I going to do?
This bucket of bolts, has got to last,
It's me or it, that goes on a fast.

Goody's through checking, his expression's bland,
But is that a calculator, he has in hand?
His educated fingers, they certainly fly.
If he don't stop soon, I know I'll just die.

The moment of decision, is now at hand.
Can I pay the ransom, that they demand?
The bottom price, that Goody has set,
Sounds more to me, like the National Debt!

These beads of sweat, here on my brow.
How short of breath, I seem somehow.
My hand's a-tremble, the pen I grab it,
And mortgage my life, for my *WHEELIE* habit.

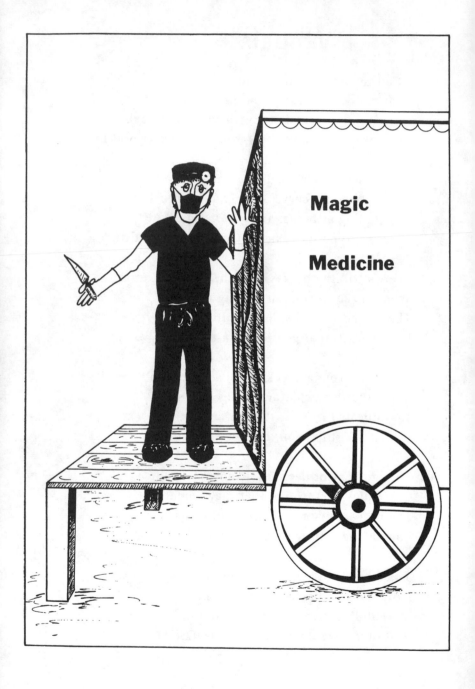

MEDICINE

20

Achoo

Of Medical Clinics, there's quite a boom,
With an innovation, in the waiting room.
This dismal area, in days of yore,
Now features toys, all over the floor.

Toys for the tots, to lick and chew,
Exchange some *viruses,* and *bacteria* too.
Regardless of why, the tot was there,
He'll probably be back, for further repair.

There's toys at home, at Play-School too,
To spread the germs, so through and through.
Then why place more, and, of ALL places,
On Waiting Room Floors, to get in kid's faces.

Waiting Rooms of old, they were a bore,
And the fretful kids, did bawl and roar.
But the only germs, old Doc did stem,
Were those kids brought, along with them.

'Twas a good idea, the kids to amuse,
But kids are there, for germs to *LOSE!*
Toys that are shared, where germs abound.
Will certainly spread, those germs around.

Clipboarditis

The Angel of Mercy, Gift of the Lord,
Has fallen *prey* to, the ubiquitous clipboard.
Press the *NURSE* button, you get in her stead,
A *disembodied voice,* from back of the bed.

Your light interupts, her duty so consTANT,
Filling her clipboards, with data imporTANT.
Data to clue in, the physicians galore,
Who have but minutes, to *cover the floor.*

Data that's fed to, that monstorous computer.
Nary a patient *charge,* dares to elude 'er.
Oh, data for this-a, and even for that'a,
She's a clipboard jockey, riding herd on data.

Let the new trainee, shuffle out pills,
Anyone have time, Room 203 has chills.
The writer's cramp drives, her out'a her mind,
Yet as of now, she's six boards behind.

Oh, that signal light, for room two-o-four,
He'll have to wait, a little while more.
It's three more clipboards, and then to lunch,
If his light bothers you, just give it a *PUNCH.*

Eeny — Meeny — Miny — Mo --

There's a hue and cry, throughout the land,
That medical costs, are out of hand.
Oh, there's little doubt, their howl is just,
Uncle and Insurers, might soon go bust.

Get a second opinion, the Sages advise.
Opinion, schimion! To nobody's surprise,
The mumbo-jumbo spoken, by that profession,
Is in latin and Greek! Seems an obsession.

For openers, you'll note, there's three divisions.
A selection is among, your first decisions.
Is it *Snip* or *Zap,* or just *Medication.*
For each will suggest, his own specialization.

The Surgeon, for sure, wants to *Snip* it out.
A Radium or Laser man, his *Zap* will tout.
Or a *Pill and Needler,* will his chemicals push,
Either down your gullet, or into your tush.

A *Snipper* a *Zapper,* or a *P and N.*
Chances of choosing right, are about one in ten.
Old Solomon himself, no decision could make,
But you are asked, this decision to take.

Why not a Computer, with an '800' phone,
To hear your symptoms, all that are known.
And then in a language, that we all understand,
List the best treatment, that's now on hand.

Armed with this info., you're now in position,
To discuss the subject, with any physician.
And a second won't match, the first diagnosis,
itis for itis, and *osis for osis.*

A *Snip* or *Zap,* or *Medication* indeed,
May be exactly, just what you need.
But if you know, the latest treatMENT.
You won't wind up, so financially BENT!

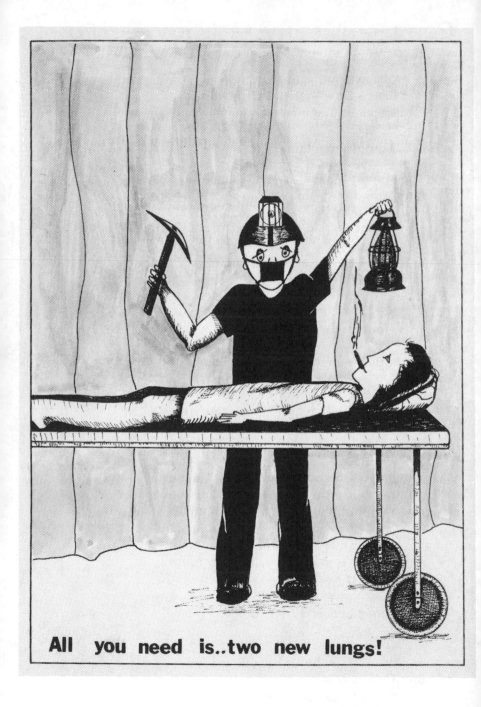

All you need is..two new lungs!

Pity your poor lung

Naught in the world, like a cigarette.
Naught, this is, your life to upset.
Devote yourself, to that hazy smoke,
Chances are good, you may just choke.

There's hair that line, the tubes of your lung.
Cilia they're called, from Latin it sprung.
There's muscles that move, these cilia wise,
The garbage you suck in, they hate and dispise.

These cilia will fight, with lots of clout.
If ash you breath in, they brush it back out.
But cilia do wear, and finally turn off,
Turning the job over, to that *CIGARETTE COUGH.*

As a back-up system, the cough will do,
Until, that is, the tubes go too.
With walls worn thin, the tubes will collapse.
And the garbage is trapped, not just perhaps!

The surgeons will probe, or maybe excise.
And hidden therin, is where cancer lies.
Then the *Therapy Twins,* both Radium and Chemo,
Will make your life, just touch and go.

When for every breath, you gasp and choke,
You'll wonder why, you had to smoke.
If the scenerio above, seems awfully grim,
You'll soon be able, to complain to Him.

If you see yourself, falling in this trough.
The cilia gone, and starting to cough,
It's not too late, the course to stop.
JUST QUIT BREATHING IN, THAT HORRIBLE SLOP!

28

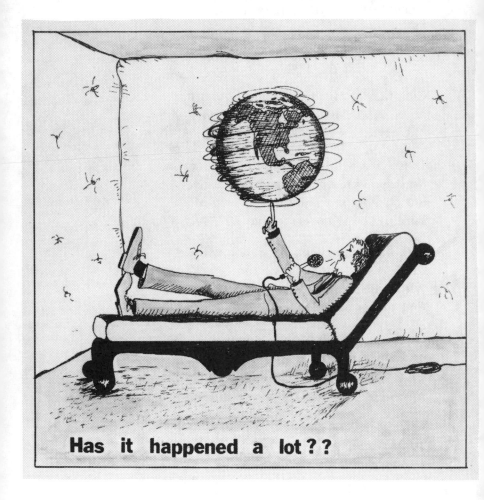

Psychiatry on the Air

Would'st bare your soul, both far and wide?
Expose your ego, your prejudice, your pride?
Just dial the number, of your Radio Station,
An Electronic Psychiatrist, will inform the nation.

Unlimber your problems, your deepest woes,
Your sexual fantasies, yes, even those!
If you beat your mate, or don't have a friend,
Then tell the whole world, from end to end.

Your blackest secrets, that you used to hide,
Are now broadcast, the air waves to ride.
Wonder if Marconi, in his invention foresaw,
Such violent emotions, and nerves so raw?

What possible effect, has this wide exposure,
On the nervous wretch, who's making the disclosure?
A Radio Psychiatrist, is as good, every bit,
As a do-it-yourself, brain surgery kit.

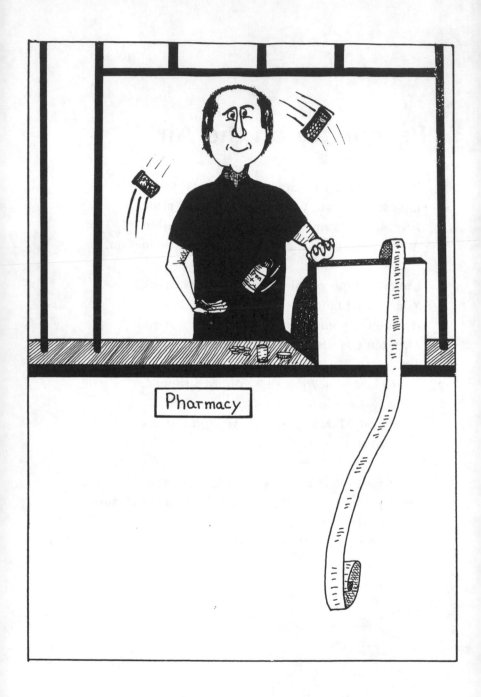

Pharmacy

Your Phriendly Pharmacist

Breathes there a soul, who dosen't dread,
To their phriendly, pharmacist to head,
With slip of latin scratchin', by old Doc's hand,
So hastily scratched, in hieroglyphics grand.

An interpreter there, the code will decipher,
His utter frustration, you can't help but sigh for.
The walls of the cubical, in which he's enclosed,
Holds zillions of pills, —could be any of those.

There's oceans of lotions, and elixers galore,
Batches of patches, from ceiling to floor.
There's even a mortar, and a pestle too,
That ain't been used, since 19 aught 2.

On a recent prescription, he could only make out,
A dandruff shampoo, and this was for gout!
But wonder of wonder, he fathoms them all,
Even for stones, both kidney and gall.

Oh, it's pills he counts, for hour upon hour,
Some coated with sugar, some awfully sour.
But the bitterest pills, he'll hand out today,
Are the register slips, that you'll pay—and pay—

MARKETS

Click, Click, Click — Whir-r-r

A brand new way, for groceries to pay,
Checks and cash are, no longer Oh Kay.
The Grocer now sticks, an electronic paw,
Into your Bank Account, and makes a draw.

Before your groceries, are in the bag,
Your Bank Account, will feel the sag.
No rubber checks, or three-dollar bills,
Will find their way, into grocers tills.

No *Paper Hangers,* will ply their trade,
And *No Funds checks,* from sight will fade.
The Grocer will smile, from ear to ear,
And his cash-flow problems, may disappear.

But what of customers, who ever of yore,
Had trouble in balancing, their checks galore.
With but a slip, their account to adjust,
Reconciliations will, be cussed and cussed.

And *all other checks,* both before and after,
May bounce and bounce, up to the rafter.
While the electronic transfer, the Grocer has used,
Finds cash in the account, or the groceries refused.

With Electronic Transfer, and groceries Scanned,
The Grocer's problems, seem well in hand.
But his next idea, your mind just staggers,
Super electronic, Checkers and Baggers!

In the Arms of Morpheus

New Motels and Hotels, spring up like mushrooms,
And private home owners, now offer their rooms.
But the latest boudoirs, they are really unique,
Are not slept in, by the upper clique.

These novel accommodations, of which we speak,
Don't rent by the day, or month, or week.
In fact they're free, and even *plentiful,*
And sleeping in them, can be, *event-i-ful!*

To avail oneself, of these sleeping facilities,
One has need of, certain physical agilities.
A six-foot climb, and a monsterous cover,
You must negotiate, this bed to discover.

No need to register, or leave a call,
Reservations are never, a problem at all.
Just lift the lid, and climb right in,
The large commercial, *DUMPSTER TRASH BIN.*

A word of caution! You should sleep light,
And keep the dump truck, always in sight.
It's not the slide, that dumps you in,
But the *COMPACTOR,* that'll press you thin.

A couple of roomers, have now been dumped,
And one *compacted,* bruised and lumped.
Sanitary Engineers! Please dump with care.
There's just no telling, who's sleeping in there!

King-sized

There passing was sad, we knew them well,
But *MEDIUM* and *SMALL,* they do not sell.
LARGE is still around, but it's been demoted,
LARGE is now *SMALL,* it should be noted.

There's four sizes bigger, it's hard to believe,
KING, GIANT & FAMILY, we readily perceive.
But let's not forget, the *LARGE ECONOMY SIZE,*
That may cost more per ounce. Surprise?

Now size is often, an illusion we vow,
Its outer appearance, don't show somehow,
The air sealed in, or empty space,
A bottom that's false, the product to replace.

If we could eat, the card-board we buy,
We'd need but half, the food so high.
Most everything's wrapped, its size to conceal,
And then played up, as a wonderful deal!

The weight's they list, are mostly fractions,
To figure their cost, needs drastic actions.
A shopper wise, will a calculator carry,
And frustrate those Packers, who's weights so vary.

Oh, Shopping for food, is a battle of wits.
The tricks they use, give one the *FITS*.
But then, *ALL* precaution, is to no avail,
Everthing you buy, is a ***CHEMICAL COCKTAIL.***

Nice Day

"Have a nice day". "Have a nice day".
A thousand and one, times today!
But the mood, I'm in, I'd rather frown.
The way I feel, is down
          down
            down

My set of wheels, is in the shop.
My stereo chose, today to stop.
But "Have a nice day", says this clown.
When even my stock, is down
          down
            down

My nag at the track, he came in last,
The rent on my pad, is due and past.
But it's, "Have a nice day", all over town.
S'Help me, I'll mow, the whole lot down
              down
                down

If one more "Have a nice day" I hear,
From a face that's grinning, from ear to ear.
That lout, you can bet, I'll just crown,
Then blow, yes, blow-w-w the man down
              down
                down

Where's the package that you wanted open ?

Packaged for your protection

If ever they drop, those bombs of Hydrogen.
There's one safe place, to hide from them.
Just wrap yourself, from hat to shoes,
In that *FANTASTIC PLASTIC,* the Packagers use.

That plastic's so strong, it's really kid-proof.
Couldn't be dented, if dropped from a roof.
Maybe an *Air Hammer,* or *Acid Muriatic,*
Would chip or melt, this *substance erratic.*

Every instrument pointed, in the average home,
From Florida's last Key, to Alaska's Nome,
From California's Coronado, to the tip of Maine,
Is dull from jabbing, *and jabbing in vain!*

Every knife, every blade, every shovel, every spade,
Are dull or broken. The plastic? It stayed!
When all else fails, you can stop the strife,
Go to the Fire House, for a *JAWS OF LIFE!*

Adding insult to injury, only package has in,
Ten times your need, for the items therein.
Nothing these days, in a package of one.
The Customer as usual, is kicked in the bun!

Pity the Cashier

Lo, the Inventory, that old bug-a-bear,
Caused many a Boss, to tear his hair.
But this ancient rite, was ever heretofore,
Done out back, in the bowels of the store.

By knots on a rope, or an abacus rare,
Or Accountants astride, a high Clark's chair.
A scratchy quill pen, the totals recorded,
So an annual figure, could be duly recorded.

But all this changed, in the computer age.
The Accountant's gone, from his hidden cage.
Year-end inventories, we no longer hold,
The count is changed, with each item sold!

And how, you ask, does this magic occur?
Just watch the cashier, her *fingers a blur.*
Punching *forty-leven keys,* for each item sold,
As a Robot in back, the totals enfold.

But what of customers, an *impatient throng,*
Standing in line, *half a mile long?*
They gripe, they grumble, in sad dismay,
And the cashier advises, "Have a nice day"!

Up and Off

The hottest sales gimmick, in the retail game?
An adverb and an adjective, plus a little shame.
The adverb is *UP,* and the adjective is *OFF,*
But to the unwary, they're a cheap *RIP-OFF.*

In large bold letters, an amount is stated,
The *PRICE* is right! The customer is baited.
What wasn't noticed, and in letters small,
Is *UP* or *OFF,* and the suckers fall.

The actual price, on a hidden price tag,
If found and noted, will beat the gag.
But some will toss it, into their cart,
And count themselves, as shoppers smart.

If the bill is large, at the store check-out,
The actual price, may never come out.
And if it does, they'll take it, you know,
For buyers are ashamed, their ignorance to show.

It's mean, it's low, shame on the users.
And all of the *CHAINS,* are the worst abusers.
This is the same, as *BAIT AND SWITCH,*
Thought up by a smart, --- -- - -----!

48

Where's the Checkout?

Drivel and Trivia, on racks galore.
Drivel to the ceiling, trivia to the floor.
But where, oh where, is the check-out stand?
All that I want, is my groceries scanned.

Magazines in racks, and books in stacks,
There's gum, cigarettes and hosiery in packs.
But it's for a check-out stand, *I'M* looking,
Not books by the thousands, on outdoor cooking.

There's candy delights, at kid-finger heights,
High-flying kites, and Christmas tree lights.
But somewhere beneath, this super sales hype,
There must be a check-out, the *OLD FASHIONED TYPE.*

The displays grow thicker, the racks close in.
My basket won't fit, the aisle's too thin.
But if really this is, the check-out stand,
Then Lord have mercy, on *BUDGETS PLANNED.*

SPACE

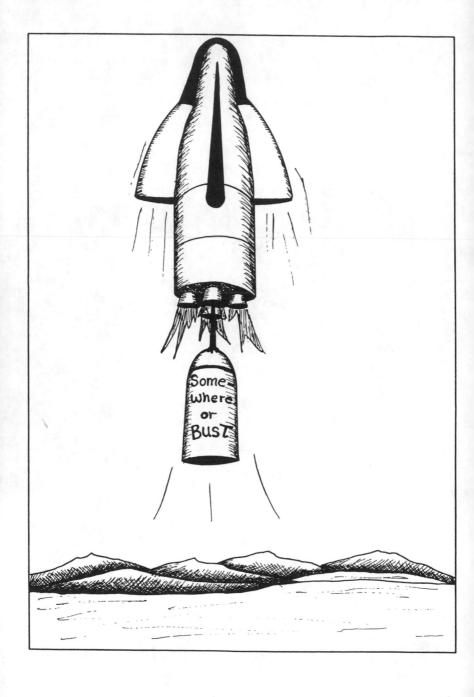

All-l-l Abo-o-o-oard

All aboard! For space Station One.
Who'll be ready, when construction's done?
Who is prepared, this planet to depart,
And live your life, on a *WHIRLING GO-CART.*

Does a closed ecology, appeal to you?
Tired of old Earth, that planet so blue?
Will your brain retrain, and your psyche adjust,
Are you ready to sate, your wonderlust?

The tickets, of course, are one-way only,
Don't come aboard, if ever you're lonely.
Our destination's, the distant stars,
We won't even stop, on nearby *MARS.*

We're off to circle, some distant Sun,
Preferably one, who's life's just begun.
No. We haven't, of our minds been bereft,
But earth has only, *FOUR BILLION YEARS LEFT!*

We'll keep in touch, for a few light years,
Or the fiftieth century, if first, it appears.
And ease your mind, should the *BOMB* arrive,
This bit of humanity, will surely survive.

Comet Comment

Hello out there Stranger. Old Comet named Halley
Long time no see, down here in our alley.
Seventy-six years, since your previous visit,
Not very neighborly, of you, now is it?

How's things out there, on Pluto and Neptune?
Or were they away, when past you did zoom?
How's Uranus and Saturn, with their moons galore?
That red spot on Jupiter, that looks so sore?

What's new on Mars, or in the Asteroid Belt?
Perhaps in passing, their pulse you felt.
Now here on Earth, it just ain't the same,
Since nineteen-ten, *it's a new ball game!*

Many folks once thought, you a demon not nice,
Where now we feel, you're a big chunk of ice.
We even considered, coming out to explore,
But ice we've got, here on Earth galore.

We admire your tail, flying the solar wind,
And later on when, to your nose it's pinned.
We'd like to visit, and probe your gizzards,
But we can't afford, to pay *NASA'S* wizards.

So make your turn, and head back out,
Your old black magic, has lost its clout.
You're lucky we hadn't, the rockets in tubes,
To come on out, and chop you into *CUBES.*

Say hello to the gang, of planets out there,
Warn them now for, Homo Sapiens to prepare.
Old Planet Earth's crowded, and room we need,
Yea, soon we'll be, on a planet-hopping steed.

So fly your ordbit, Oh, chunk so frozen,
Come twenty-sixty-one, we may not be dozin'.
We could be lurking, somewhere in Space,
And clamber all over, your *COLD ICY FACE.*

U.F.O.'s

Oh, some say yes, but nobody knows,
The subject in doubt. Are there UFOs?
Those that see 'em are very specific,
Those that don't, protest terrific.

Some not only see, man, they ride 'em.
And state in detail, just what's inside 'em.
They even describe, the creatures therein,
Who all seem to wear, antennas thin.

The creatures too, are all super-human.
Compared to them, we're idiots bloomin'.
With just ESP, your mind they decipher,
Your whole life's history, is what they try for.

The ships are odd, their shapes are weird.
Cigars or saucers, and cosmic geared.
Most all cruise, at the speed of light,
Blink your eye, and they're *out of sight*.

Oh, the UFOs, their beholders amaze,
A ride in one, sure your mind would daze.
Creatures so smart, and so very clever,
Land here in Atom-Bomb-Alley? *NO. NEVER!*

AROUND THE HOUSE

Button, button

A remote control, for our new T.V.
Hangs in the bathroom, the reason you'll see.
As the announcer ups, the pitch's volume,
We're in a position, to counter-act the bum.

He thinks he's smart, you'll hear him speak,
Though you have fled, some relief to seek.
A button in there, to tone him down,
Sure serves him right, the sneaky clown.

There's another button, at the kitchen sink
Where oft we go, for another drink.
His screaming voice, heard there of yore,
It won't be heard, there any more!

The remote I want, oh, it's a honey,
Can not be had, for love or money.
For it turns down, a Hi-Fi or T.V.
In that apartment, next door to me.

Exodus

People and Businesses, how they did run,
From snow and taxes, and into the Sun.
Threw in the sponge, gave up the fight,
Saved a few dollars, and beat winter's bite.

Pitched out their longies, at Dixie's Line,
Impatient to enjoy, that great sunshine.
Counted their savings, from taxes and fuel,
Bought bakinis to swim, in an outdoor pool.

When all are there, every Son and Daughter,
Lord only knows, where they'll get water.
In flimsy houses, and Temp. at one-ten,
They'll miss lake breezes, of way back then.

Those savings envisioned, for housing will go,
And quakes and shakes, their minds will blow.
In those terrible snows, like winter Eighty-five,
Some will be lucky, to get out alive.

They'll miss the services, that taxes pay,
Such as the snow plows, to clear the way.
Lo, that green, green grass, that we ever sense,
Over on the other, side of the fence.

The discordant cord

It's not how much, a Wood Chuck chucks,
But how much wood, cost how many bucks.
For wood is sold, by a measure antique,
A **CORD** it's called, to add some mystique.

The sellers of wood know, of buyers new.
There'll always be, but a mighty few,
Who knows the volume, a cord should contain.
So every cord, is whatever they maintain.

Four feet by four feet, and eight feet long,
It says in the dictionary, who's seldom wrong.
That four feet wide, can be two, even one.
Thus a **FACED** cord, and you've been done.

Soft wood's cheap and, a poor heat source,
Hard wood may cost, it's better, of course.
Burn soft, and your chimney it'll coat,
With creosote, a fire-hazard you'll note.

A cord of hard wood, is heavy indeed.
Two or three tons. This message heed.
If delivered to you, on one pick-up truck.
Needless to say, you've really been stuck.

To sum it all up, unless time's been done,
Out on a farm, or you're an Abe Lincoln.
With cords of wood, do not yourself embroil.
Far better you should, burn gas or oil.

The Mad Mower

A slave at oar, on a Roman Trireme
Was no more slave, at least it would seem
Than an owner proud, with grass so green,
Chained so tightly, to his mowing machine.

A three-decked Galley, during the battle's roar,
Made no more noise, than his power mower.
With horse-power enough, to pull a plow,
He mows off an inch, every then and now.

If only he'd go, and chase a white pill,
Chasing it madly, o'er dale and hill.
Or maybe go feed, some worms to a fish.
But neither of these, are really his dish.

He'll work half nude, sweat like a Trojan,
Much harder by far, than any slave Roman.
His whole world seems, just Roar and Green,
Chained so tightly, to his mowing machine.

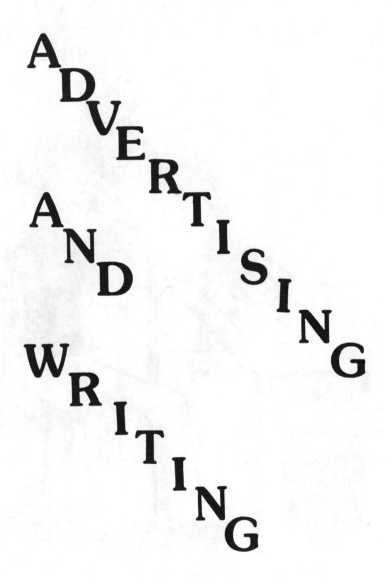

Courting the Muse

He, who would write, the Muse must court.
When words seem trite, but time is short.
With a dead-line near, or a cupboard bare,
While upon a sheet, so blank, you stare.

At first you ponder, and then meditate.
You stare out yonder, or curse your fate.
Maybe grind your teeth, maybe drum the table,
But words won't come, you just ain't able.

You stir the computer, the one in your head,
Gears are ka-poot or, the battery dead.
You tug on an ear, wipe your hot brow,
There's nothing, no where, no way, no how.

It's just no use, you lay back, relax.
And there is the *MUSE,* with facts and facts.
You scribble and scratch, or type pell-mell,
And condem the Muse, to rot in Hell!

But words flow smooth, ideas, they pop,
The text inspired, the words won't stop.
A *FLASH* from above, your hand does guide,
The Muse is really, your friend inside.

Evermore

The joys of December, come but once a year.
Other months limp, along in low gear.
What the economy needs, is three more shots,
Of Christmas type hype, aimed at the tots.

Say an Ethan Allen, on a charger white,
Galloping o'er roof tops, on a moonlit night.
Saddlebags packed, with oodles of toys,
Gifts for the kiddies, from Green Mountain Boys.

And down the chimney, in the parlor below
A Liberty Bell hung, with the crack to show.
And room beneath, for presents galore.
DECEMBER IN JULY, AND SALES EVERMORE.

Next then in sight, is Christopher C.
Dodging the chimneys, in the Santa Marie.
His winch and boom, unloading the loot,
Of toys and gifts, then off he'll scoot.

Down in the Rec. Room, in holiday array
Are Nina and Pinta, with anchors a-weigh.
Their decks a-wash, in presents galore.
DECEMBER IN OCTOBER, AND SALES EVERMORE.

O'er the roof-tops worn, in a two-wheel cart,
Drawn by leprechauns, in a manner smart.
There's still St. Paddy, with potato-bag of toys,
To dump down the chimney, for wee girls and boys.

'Neath shamrocks hung, on the mantle with care,
To show the kiddies, St. Paddy's been there.
Are presents and presents, and presents galore.
DECEMBER IN MARCH, AND SALES EVERMORE.

Santa, Chris, Paddy and Allen's, roof-top flight
Will rattle cash registers, from morning till night.
The economy'll boom, that's if Mom and Dad,
Don't ever *discover,* how they've *been had!*

Exposé

Oh why, oh why? Are we so want,
The High and Mighty, to tear and taunt?
Now a Magazine, it will not sell,
Unless a *NAME*, it rips to Hell!

If an Editor you ask, for what he'll pay.
His answer's easy. A good Exposé!
We've fallen in, up to our necks,
An In - fer - ior, i - ty Complex.

We hold ourselves, so very, very low,
Our egos have suffered, from blow after blow.
Till the only way, for our egos to rise,
Is to bring someone *BIG*, down to our size.

Our heroes of old, who's deeds we've known,
Have all been pulled, down off their throne.
No name, no face, no deed so great,
A rip-snorting exposé, can't den-i-grate!

Would that we spend, our writing skills,
On something uplifting, not character kills.
Let's polish our writing, that *WE* gain fame,
And stop tearing down, another's good name!

Have you been M.A.D.'d today?

We all battle M. A., the live-long day,
Madison Avenue, that is, to say.
The Pitch, the Gimmick, the Come-on, the Hype,
From peanuts to pickles, from tacos to tripe.

The packages scream, they brag, they boast,
But it's Ads, you know, that cost the most.
SAVE THIRTY DOLLARS, the big Ads advise,
Bunk and Baloney, that's naught but lies.

The *SAVINGS* they claim, are only a ruse,
Who would believe them, not even a goose.
The food's all *hyped,* and priced out of sight,
To pay for the Ads, and containers so bright.

The Ads are BIG, the Ads are BOLD,
Everthing SOUNDS, as good as gold.
A SUPER-DUPER SOUP, an INCREDIBLE EGG.
Don't be a sucker, they're pulling your leg.

Be a shopper wise, for gimmicks look out,
The bigger the Ad, the stiffer the clout.
Shop and compare, and the hype ignore,
And take more money, home from the store.

Humor

Oh, tell us not, in numbers mournful,
Why T.V. comedy, is now so pornful.
Why no Skeltons, and why no Bennys.
Where the Magees, and one-liner Hennys.

This taste for mirth, so down to earth
A back-room bar, must give it birth.
One gag per second, all sexually explicit.
From the laugh machine, a guffaw will elicit.

Is sex so funny, so all-fired amusing?
Humor and Porno, they may be confusing.
The laughs, the snickers, who's to decide?
May be embarrassment, they're trying to hide.

Material to be funny, needn't be foul.
Humor of old, brought a bigger howl.
The hey-day of humor, on the T. and V.
Was censored just enough, for all to see.

A cleaned up act, is what's called for.
Dial out the trash, and then what's more.
If the dirt don't stop, turn off the set.
When enough of us have, it'll stop, you bet!

RESTAURANTS

No wonder I hate to cook !

Dished out

Breakfast at home? No way! Obsolete!
Easier by far, to go out and eat.
No pots and pans, no dirty dishes,
No dishpan hands, from detergents vicious.

An egg's an egg, and an order of toast,
Taste like home, or at least almost.
Hashed browns and bacon, your taste buds delight,
With no greasy skillet, or grill to fight.

Flapjacks or bisquits, with syrup a-plenty,
Toast ala French, and sausage scenty.
They all taste better. Know what I mean?
With dishes all washed, and by a machine.

The Markets all scream, their sales are down.
As Restaurants spring up, all over town.
Those groceries will lay, on the Grocer's shelves,
Unless those dishes, learn to wash themselves.

Garcon'

Where has she gone, that living doll?
The Waitress who stood, at our beck and call?
Her pad in hand, to list our wishes,
That the menu said, were available dishes.

So attentive she, to our every question,
Her very manner, helping our digestion.
To suggest an entree, unless we inquired,
Wouldn't have occured, to this maid inspired.

This kind of Service, is now de trop.
The Manager has hired, some one with *GO*.
A Salesperson it said, in the newspaper Ad.
To sell his food, and sell it like mad.

The *WAITRESS* now hits, your table side,
Armed to the teeth, with selections wide.
Would you like a juice? A rasher of bacon?
How about hash-browns? Or bisquits we're makin'?

Care for a drink? A dish of hors d'oeuvres?
And on and on, they pound your nerves.
A different wine, with each new course.
You no, no, no, till you're almost hoarse.

The pitch goes on, with such endurance,
They must, in the past, have sold insurance.
Theirs but to do, not to reason why,
For if they don't, it's just good-bye.

Given his way, the owner, of course,
Will fatten us up, as big as a horse.
It used to be, a gastronomical delight.
But it's *battle of the bulge,* we now must fight.

Le Grand Cuisine

Of all the places, we go to eat,
A Cafeteria's, our favorite retreat.
The diners that eat, at a serving spot,
Buy, sight unseen. A trusting lot.

Whereas we characters, who wait in line,
We want to see it, for e'er we dine.
We eat therefore, in a Cafeteria,
Where sights you see, will often cheer ya'.

The diners there, though in for a meal,
Quite often appear, en des'habill'e.
Some would appear, on a picnic bound,
While others seem ready, to work the ground.

The meals they assemble! A gourmet would cry.
A Dietician'd be wishin', that she could die.
The average notion, of a balanced meal,
Is keeping the tray, on an even keel.

Cafeteria dining, is quite an education,
Watching human nature, at a feeding station.
Where only the heft, of the diner's bill-fold,
Dictates the amount, his stomach will hold.

In the Cafeteria line, there's much gray hair.
And many a many, huge derriere.
The menu won't feature, pate de foie gras.
The diner's the goose, with the avoirdupois!

So characters arise! Stand up for your rights!
Eat what you want! Enjoy the sights!
Oh now, haut cuisine, is for the elite,
But not for us, we *like to eat!*

HUMAN
NATURE

Batter up

Under the blazing, mid day Sun,
Stands the Ump., a mighty one.
His face of stone, hid by a mask,
His body braced, to bear his task.

His job to rule, these motley nines,
Call strikes and balls, and scan foul lines.
To watch for balks, and deliveries tricky,
And catch the balls, with hair grease sticky.

His practiced eye, a strike must call.
Though batter, manager, and crowd scream *BALL!*
The rules are myriad, the players devious.
And oft they act, in a manner grevious.

The play is close, the runner is out.
Manager and Player, go into a pout.
Both do a dance, their arms they flail.
The Ump. just stares, he's tough as a nail.

He allows this scene, the excitement to enhance.
Then slowly his eyes, toward the showers glance.
As if by magic, calm is restored.
His threat to banish, dare not be ignored.

The game is close, the chips are down.
His call now against, this tough home town.
So bottles and cushions, by fans are thrown,
And the Ump's ancestry, *declared unknown!*

The Manger kicks dust, on Ump's shined shoes.
Opposing players, each other abuse.
A melee erupts, some blows are thrown,
Injuries are slight, not one broken bone.

The final scores, are of little import.
It's not who won, in this National Sport.
What's really involved? Was it wild or tame.
In this, America's, *BEST BELOVED GAME!*

Compo Sapiens

Standing in the offing, the computer that thinks.
For real, not just, Scientific hi-jinks.
A replacement for, the present Homo-Sapiens?
That's you and me, our relatives and friends!

It seems that we, flesh, bones and glands,
Are but a step, in Evolution's plans.
When Comp Sapiens, the Earth does walk,
Of aches and pains, he need not talk.

But here now exists, an opportunity grand.
In reforming the race, let's take a hand.
A micro-chip here, a macro-chip there,
And correct the ills, that we had to bear.

A chip for sure, and welded in place,
To avoid Compo's over, producing the race.
And several chips, for the elimination
Of wars and riots, crime and discrimination.

With Compo perfected, Space we can ply.
Turn off his current, let the Space ship fly.
Wake him each century, the course to stay,
As dozens of light-years, he whiles away.

While Compo may think, he will not emote.
So no one Compo, on another will dote.
No tender emotions, no marital strife.
Me thinks they'll lead, a dull, dull life!

Man

Man wants but little, here below.
A famous poet, once told us so.
Me thinks that man, way down deep,
Just wants a little, more to keep.

It ain't the loot, for which you scratch,
It's that percent, IRS doth snatch.
It ain't the wage, which seems just right,
Until the SSI, takes another bite.

And then the insurance, and other de-ducts,
Leaves the bottom line, with very few bucks.
If man wants, but little, here below,
That's exactly what, his pay-check doth show.

Out Damned K

Oh, the KKK, in the USA.
Ain't no way, like the KKK.
That off to the East, doth lay.
And is fortunately, so far away.

There's been Khadafi, and also Khomeini
And now we add, yet another meany.
One Gorbachev, known as Mikhail,
He at the head, of the Kremlin detail.

Now three K's would, seem a plenty, Nyet?
But there we have, a fourth one yet.
That's just too many, our mind is set.
Out damned K, from the alphabet!

Out! Out, we say! We'll just use a C.
If that won't work, we'll try QUE.
A letter that makes, for so much mischief,
Can go get lost, who'll notice the diff'.

We've twenty-five more, who all behave.
You won't be missed, you troublesome knave.
And as you leave, please take along,
Those couple of groups, so very wrong!

POSSLQ's

Step up and see, a species brand new,
With title so strange, called a POSSLQ.
And like its name, it's habitat is unique,
To seek it out, in the CENSUS you peek.

Oh some will say, it's but a euphemism.
When noses being counted, aren't Mr. and Mis'm.
The Census so tactful, would never make use
Of Shack-or and Shack-ee, those terms so obtuse.

The male of the specie, ever ready to fight,
In defense thereof, his inaleinable right.
To flaunt tradition, to thumb his nose.
Who needs a license, to hell with those.

His right to leave, he thus keeps ope'.
To flee the nest, if he can't cope.
Milleniums of customs, he'll cast aside
It's modern and smart, to seek a *free ride.*

Now the POSSLQ female, is harder to explain.
With no real advantage, for her to gain.
The *Ties that Bind,* of all history recorded,
She will gladly forego, how can she afford it?

Could be her plan, this Lover to bait,
Into marital bliss, at some future date.
But the odds are poor, for statistics show,
Even in marriage, one in two will blow.

But what of offspring, that these POSSLQs sire?
Will their parent's actions, these children admire?
Or will they feel, that missing piece of paper,
A million times preferable, to a POSSLQ caper?

Sh-h-h-h

Oh why, Oh why. Please tell me why?
A Library's so quiet? Did somebody die?
Why such an aire, of impending doom?
Why all the shushing? Sounds like a tomb.

And why the Librarian, in a whisper speaks?
Her voice never rises, her ire never peeks.
Probably goes home, and can't hardly wait
To yell and scream, for half an hour straight.

Why so subdued, and why no talking?
And what's the reason, for tip-toe walking?
A Library's a treasure, and should be enjoyed.
Here minds are stirred, and spirits buoyed.

If Libraries remain, so foreboding a place.
Few of our youth, its halls will grace.
If relaxing a little, is what we need
Then let's do it, for they've **GOT** to read.

Those who need quiet, to digest a tome,
Can charge it out, and take it home.
Let's make the Library, a place of cheer.
And maybe, just maybe, some **READERS** we'll rear.

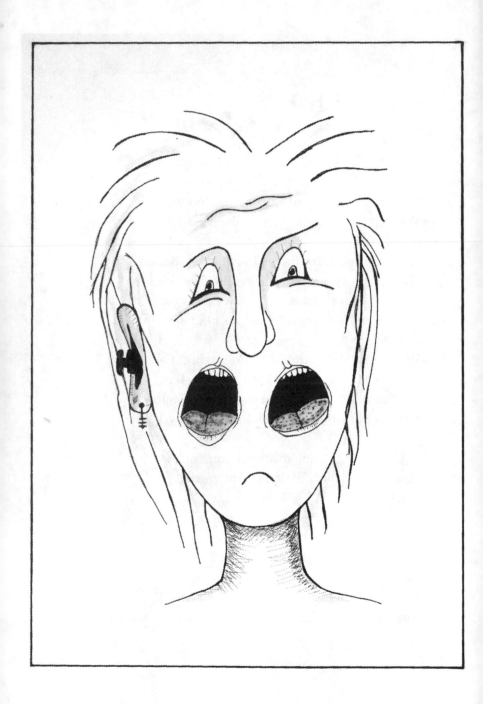

Shut up and listen

Now how could Nature, in designing man,
Have been so wrong, in a plan so grand.
Two ears, one mouth, were her decrees.
And thus she ignored, our priorities.

Just anyone knows, that **ONE** ear's enough,
To hear our fill of, the drivel and guff.
TWO mouths we need, one on each side,
To spread our knowledge, both far and wide.

Listening's a bore, we've heard it before,
And someone's always, hogging the floor.
But talking is different, it's fun, it's nice,
And particularly when, we're giving advice.

Our ears, they hurt, from the constant roar,
And interupt we must. to gain the floor.
Why do they blast, our ears without cease,
When all we want, is to speak our piece.

Interuptions ain't nice, but we all use 'em.
Some folks get mad, and won't excuse 'em.
If we didn't break in, and stop their blasting.
Why, they'd never hear, the pearls we're casting!

Tell it like it is

According to Webster, an abuser is one,
Who exceeds the amount, of what should be done.
And if nothing **SHOULD,** but yet it is,
Then the use of **ABUSER,** is just monkey bizz.

Now using **ABUSER,** when we mean **ADDICT,**
Is a euphemism, that should be kicked.
A drunk or pot-head, is not an **ABUSER,**
He is in fact, a deliberate loser.

No one forced him, on his downward path.
The decision was his, and no right he hath,
To place the blame, on some other user,
And soften his shame, saying he's an **ABUSER.**

A drunk is a drunk, a pot-head is on dope.
Listing them as **ABUSERS,** won't help them cope.
Giving them sympathy's, the last thing they need.
They're at the bottom, a back-bone is decreed.

Tell 'em like it is, if it hurts, it hurts.
Coddling them with, euphemisms is nurtz.
They're drunks and hop-heads. Tell them so.
You might get through, their **HYPED** ego.

You may convince them, that their **JUICE,**
Is not just another, little **ABUSE.**
It'll land 'em in Hell, roasting on a spit.
Then maybe, just maybe, they'll really quit!

The Talk Show Host

Women, heretofore. *ALWAYS* talked the most,
But that was before, the Talk Show Host.
All over the radio, daytime or night,
His voice drones on, the bantering trite.

Politics, Bolshevicks, talk on any level,
The Host's an Advocate, hired by the Devil.
No subject's taboo, not even a hex,
But most of the talk, is *sex, SEX, S*E*X!*

He'll argue a point, first con then pro,
With finger on button, to bleep the porno.
The Weirdos, they call, from right off the wall.
Their stories are tall, he suffers them all.

Guests give their views, they come, they go.
If your name is NEWS, then you're on the Show.
Some guests are sages, and some are schnooks,
Most common among guests, are writers of books.

Dial the Show's number, your finger grows weary,
"The subject's been changed, so sorry, old deary"
You're mad as hey-de-ho, at that son, of a witch.
But doesn't YOUR ra-di-o, have an OFF switch?

Twisters

Nothing, but nothing, can quite compare,
With old Mother Nature, out on a tear.
High on her list, of spine-chilling capers,
Are Twisters wild, those countryside rapers.

To live in an area, where Tornados spawn
Is to know real fear, when the siren is on.
That one long blast, a two-minute wail,
Will make the strongest, stop and turn tail.

Leap to the stairway, to the cellar descend.
That wind out there, can an *I-BEAM* bend.
Stop for a moment, for possessions to take.
Tomorrow your final, arrangements they'll make.

There's nothing so grim, your possessions to see,
Scattered all over, the far country.
Unless of course, it's looters and gapers.
Who read of the hit, in their evening papers.

Oh, those gaping morons, who'll drive 40 miles,
To stare dumbfounded, at junk in piles.
Or worse than that, those looters so sick.
Our utmost wish is, their *REAR ENDS TO KICK!*

"Barnum was right , there is
one born every minute!"

Wake up

You've been brain-washed! And by guess who?
THE I.R.S., no less, has done it to you.
They've scared the pants, off most Tax-Payers,
And turned them sadly, into over pre-payers.

Over with-holding, is the ransom you pay,
To keep old Uncle's, Tax Agents at bay.
Their threat to audit, gives you the *shivers,*
Just mention the word, and your body *quivers.*

Holding out too much, has nothing to do,
With whether an audit, will happen to you.
Holding out too little, is a different story.
The result can be, both costly and gory.

To hit the mark, needs no mathematician,
It's just plain fear, affecting your decision.
It's but eighty percent, you must pre-pay.
The remaining twenty, is lots of lee-way.

If you're over with-holding, some money to save,
Your financial education, is woefully *naive.*
The interest you lost, last year and a half,
Is something that makes, the tax collector laugh.

He's had your dough, and the interest too,
Saw no hurry, returning it to you.
Upon receipt, you thought it a *wind-fall?*
Does the place you live, have a *padded wall?*

In paying your taxes, some attention accord it.
Don't over-pay 'em, who can afford it?
The U.S. Treasury, is no Savings Bank.
Time to smarten up. Use your think-tank.

Wanted, a Buster

'Tis not who's who, in this 80's world,
It's who *OWNS* who, in the corporate whirl.
What once was *BIG,* is now gobbled up,
Like table scraps, by a hungry pup.

The big get bigger, the bigger, gigantic.
When will it stop, this merging so frantic?
Oh, firms so old, we thought them a fixture,
Are swallowed up whole, and out'a the picture!

A company so large, it's worth a *billion,*
Is bought by one, worth half a *trillion!*
Where does it end, this financial greed?
It could be that, upon itself it doth feed.

Sooner or later, maybe just any moMENT.
It'll all be one, and bigger'n the GovernMENT.
So what we need, and we need it bad,
Is another like **TEDDY,** that trust-buster lad.

He took 'em on, the big and the bigger,
And cut 'em to size, a reasonable *figger.*
Oh, where, oh where, shall we find his like,
For we see none such, coming down the pike.

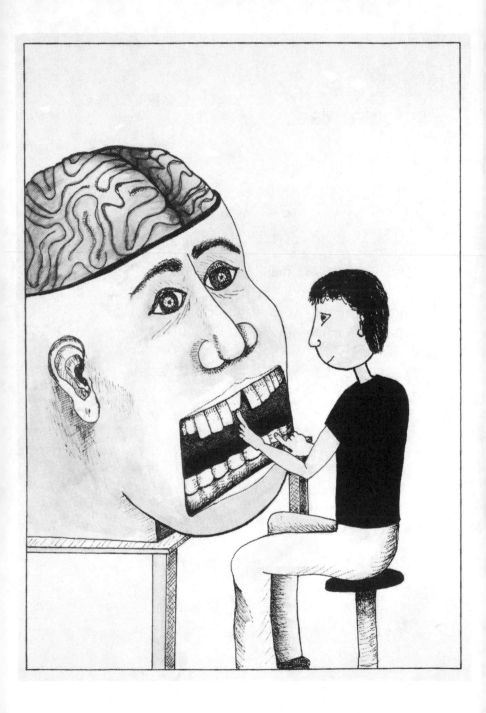

Your Billion-year-old computer

Use your computer, the one twixt your ears,
Not that gimmick, with micro-chips and gears.
The billions of cells, in your think-tank,
Will sure out-perform, the best computer bank.

A computer puts out, what someone puts in,
An original idea, sure it cannot begin.
But a computer can, an object lesson be,
Fill it with *garbage,* and *garbage* you'll see.

Your built-in *Computer,* will work the same.
What you put in, is the name of the game.
Fill up your *bank,* with drivel and trivia,
Tap it for ideas, and drivel it'll give ya!

Fill it with learning, such as the three R's,
Nourish those brain cells, all your waking hours.
And when you've need, for an idea new,
Sure now your *Computer,* will promptly come through.

You can't buy brains, try as you might.
They don't come packed, in packages bright.
Your brain's a **COMPUTER,** and truly God-given,
Program it properly, and really start livin'.

SUMMATION

And now to test the effectiveness of doggerel today — a couple of questions:

Did you learn a few facts herein that would never have been brought out by the *Media?*

Were you amused by the satire and tickled by the humor and rhyming?

If so, then doggerel has not lost its punch over the intervening centuries, but has been beaten into obscurity by *economic pressure* put upon the Media. The almighty dollar tends to pervert the meaning of *Freedom of the Press.* The Spectator newspaper and the Troubadours of 16th and 17th century England were under no such pressure.

If you enjoyed *Doggerel,* tell your friends. If not, maybe you were already *Street Smart* and didn't need it. Thanks anyway, for reading through to the last •

by george